The Shocking Shark Showdown

Read more 13th Street books!

The Shocking Shark Showdown

by **DAVID BOWLES**

illustrated by **SHANE CLESTER**

HARPER

An Imprint of HarperCollins*Publishers*

In memory of Witchy and Puchi,
the best dogs on the planet. I'll see you
on the other side. —DB

13th Street #4: The Shocking Shark Showdown
www.harperchapters.com
Library of Congress Control Number: 2020937191
ISBN 978-0-06-294789-5 — ISBN 978-0-06-294788-8 (pbk.)
Typography by Torberg Davern and Catherine Lee
20 21 22 23 24   PC/LSCC   10 9 8 7 6 5 4 3 2 1
❖
First Edition

CONTENTS

CHAPTER

FISH TANKS AND FRIENDS

For a moment, Malia stopped thinking about her plan. She just stood there, staring at the tank full of pink jellyfish.

She was at the Gulf City Aquarium with her class and teacher.

"This is our last stop!" said Ms. Garay. She pointed at the jellyfish's tentacles. "Did you know that jellyfish don't sting with electricity?

Nope! They have special cells containing poison!"

Someone giggled at Malia's side. It was Susana Leal, her best friend.

"That one looks like my brother," Susana said, smiling. "Don't you think?"

Malia nodded, forcing a laugh. Then she took a nervous breath.

A week ago, she and her cousins had decided to return to 13th Street, the monster-filled dimension they had just escaped. This field trip to the Gulf City Aquarium was the perfect moment to set their plan in motion. But they needed Susana's help.

Unfortunately, Susana had no memory of her time in 13th Street. That made everything trickier.

Dante and Ivan walked over to meet Malia. They were right on time.

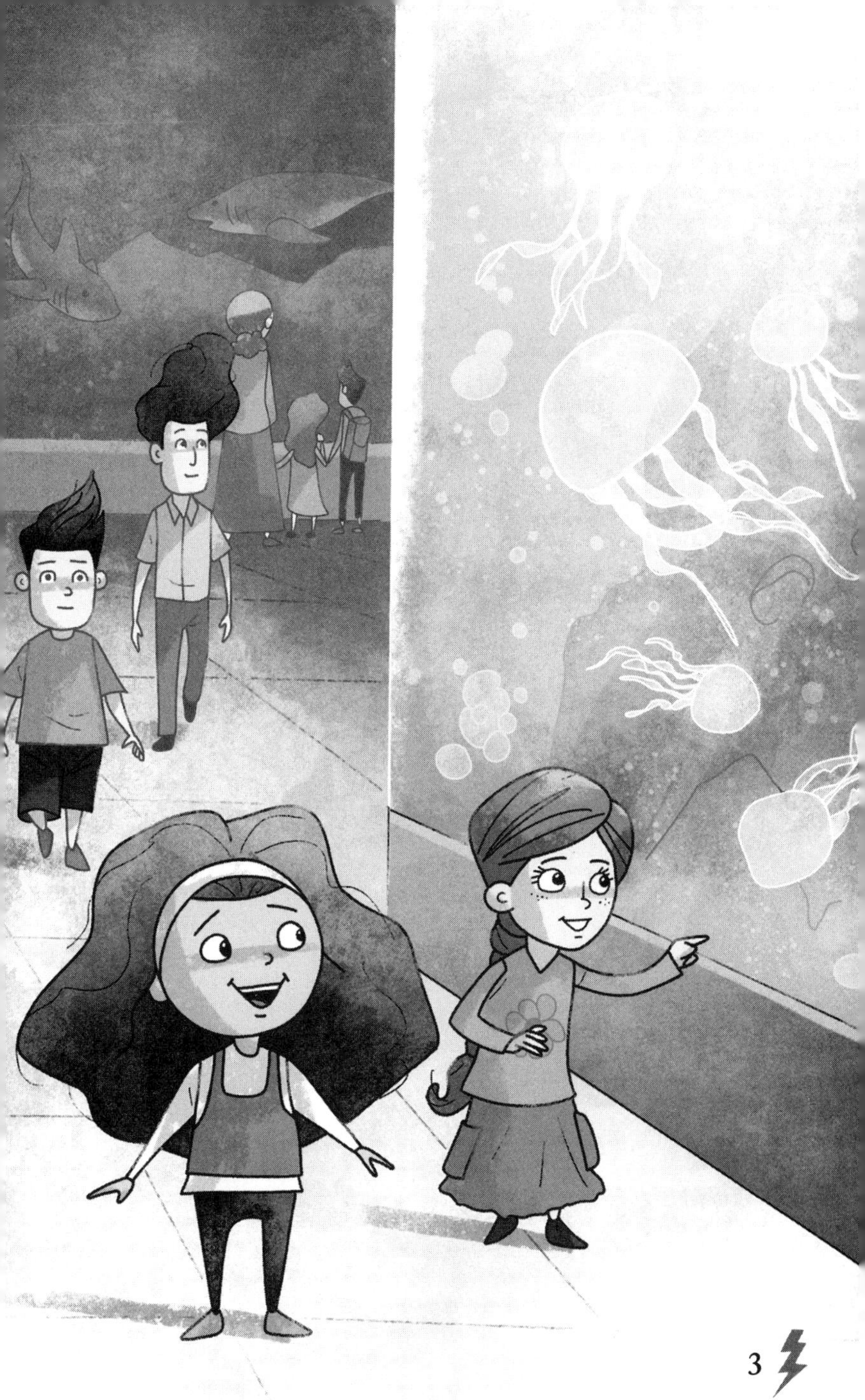

"Brains and Beauty have arrived," Dante said, smirking.

"Oh, please," muttered Susana.

Dante gave her a big grin. "Jealousy is an ugly thing, Susana."

"And now, students, free time!" Ms. Garay said excitedly, cutting off Susana's reply. "Stay

in your groups, rotating among the stations. These awesome aquarium employees can answer any questions!"

"Hey, Suse?" Malia asked. "Remember what I said on the bus?"

"You wanted to ask a favor." Susana shrugged. "I'm your BFF, Malia. Ask away!"

"Okay. I need you to cover for us. These two weirdos and me," Malia explained. "We have to go somewhere."

Susana narrowed her eyes. "Where? For how long?"

"An hour?" Malia guessed. "Maybe ninety minutes? But I can't say where."

"You can't . . . Malia, this is not cool," Susana grumbled. "We don't keep secrets from each other."

Dante sighed. "*Cómo no*. If you only knew."

Malia punched his shoulder. "It's . . . Aunt Lucy's

birthday and we want to surprise her."

Malia hated to lie to her best friend, but she didn't have a choice.

Ivan's eyes went wide. "We're getting her a pet!"

"Actually two kittens!" Dante chimed in.

Malia shot Ivan and Dante an annoyed look. *Don't overdo it!* she wanted to tell them.

"Oooh, how cute!" Susana clapped happily. "But I want receipts. Record everything on your phone, Mal. Promise?"

Feeling guiltier by the second, Malia nodded. "Yes, totally. Now, please . . . keep Ms. G distracted."

Susana looked over at their teacher, who was boring the aquarium manager with her jellyfish questions.

"*Está bien.* I've got you covered," Susana said with a wink.

CHAPTER

CHABELA'S CHOICE

As the cousins quickly slipped out the door, Malia glanced back. Susana pointed to her cell phone and mouthed the words *take pictures*. Malia gave her a thumbs-up.

In the hallway, Ivan reviewed their plan. "We go to Doña Chabela's house and talk to her. She obviously knows how to open portals, or where to find them."

"I bet she just wants her grandson to come home," Malia added. "So we're going to ask her to help send us back to 13th Street."

There was a bus stop right outside the aquarium. Within a few minutes, they were whisked into the neighborhood of Little Mexico.

There was another bus stop right on 11th Street, where both Aunt Lucy and Chabela Aguilar lived. Malia and her cousins walked away from Lucy's apartment complex as fast as they could. The last thing they needed was for her to spot them playing hooky.

The gate to Chabela's house was open. The three cousins hurried down her sidewalk and up her stairs. Malia rang the doorbell.

"Doña Chabela!" she called. "Please open up! We found your grandson!"

The door swung open almost immediately. Chabela stood there, shocked.

Then her eyes filled with tears and a huge smile spread across her wrinkled face. *"Ay, niños benditos.* You lovely children. Thank you. Please, come inside."

Her living room was full of wooden furniture and bright colors, like Lucy's apartment. But there was a sadness that Malia could feel all around her—the kind of sadness that comes when you lose something very important to you.

"We need answers, ma'am. You've tricked us into going to 13th Street three times. Why?" Malia asked.

"I'm so, so sorry," Chabela said, dropping into a chair. "Let me explain. The day I met you was the fourth anniversary of Mickey's disappearance. His parents are still looking for him, but I always believed there was something . . . supernatural at work. So that night, I prayed as hard as I could for help."

Malia noticed the house had gotten very still. Somewhere, an old clock was ticking.

"Finally, I fell asleep," Chabela continued. "And in a dream, I saw a strange woman with hair as white as bone. She told me about the entrance in the alley. 'If you want to see your grandson again,' she said, 'send a child.' When I woke up, I swore I would do no such thing. I visited the spot, found a strange shimmer in the air, and tried to step through into the Underworld. But adults can't enter."

Malia sighed. "So you sent us."

"It seemed like a sign," Chabela said, a tear running down her cheek. "You walked right

 by me on the very day Mickey had vanished. Then you returned, *gracias a Dios.* You're special."

"So you kept

sending us back," Ivan said.

"How did you know about the other two portals?" Malia asked.

"More dreams," Chabela said. "The woman with bone-white hair told me."

Dante asked, "Why didn't you just ask us for help?"

"What if you had refused?" Chabela said. "*Ay, m'ijo*, I couldn't risk it."

Ivan cleared his throat. "Well, we're here to help, Doña Chabela. Listen, Mickey is still trapped on 13th Street. He says he accidentally created it on his computer. Do you have it?"

"*Vengan*," Chabela said, gesturing for them to follow. She led them down the hall to a bedroom. It was Mickey's, Malia could tell. He had posters of famous inventors on the walls and a huge computer with three screens. In one corner was a little altar, a memorial to Bruno, with a photo of the huge Irish wolfhound above it.

Dante laced his fingers together and popped all his knuckles at once.

"I got this, guys," he said, sitting down in front of the monitors.

Malia patted him on the head. "I knew there was a reason we kept you around."

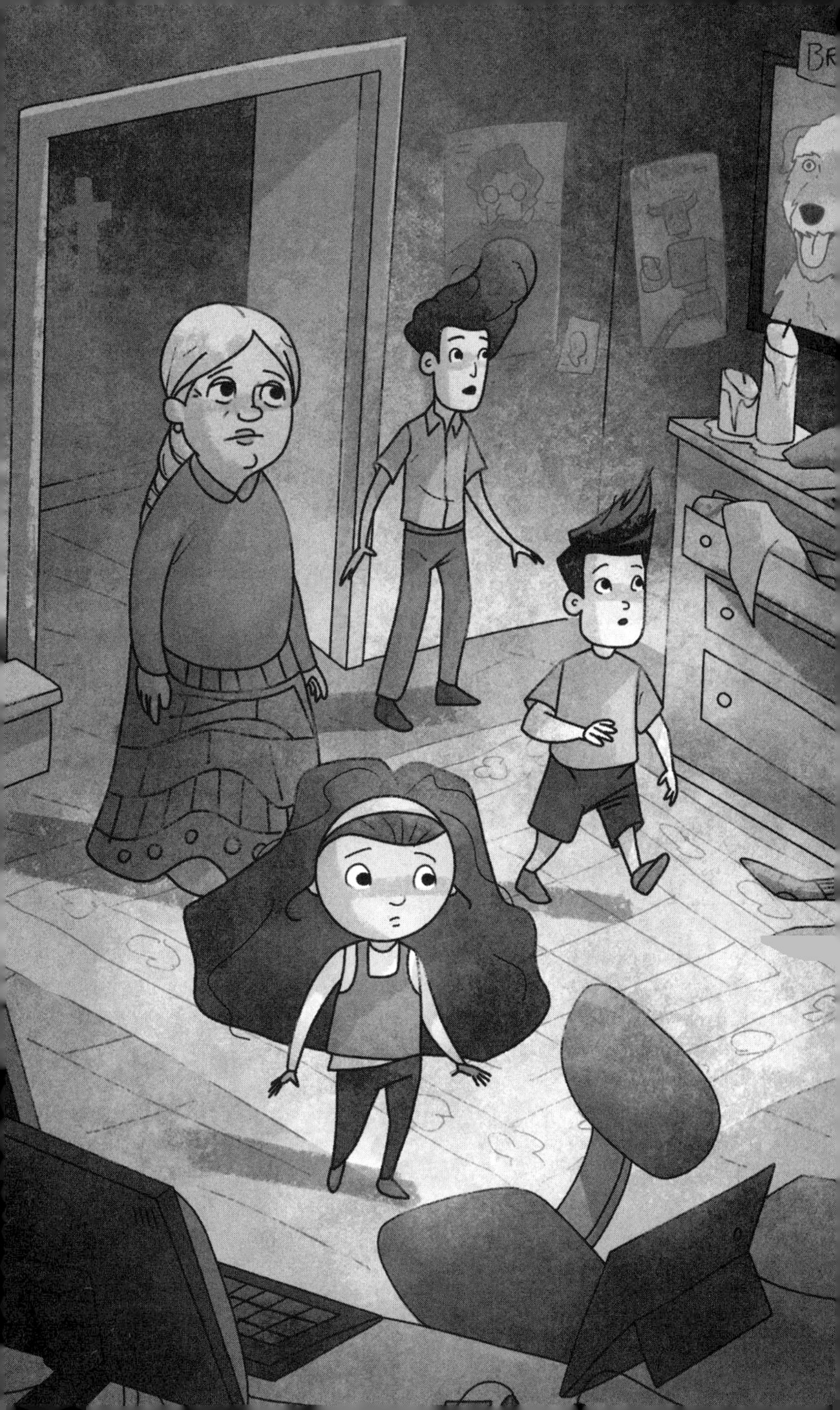

Dante started pushing buttons and keys. The screens turned on. White letters and numbers and symbols scrolled past faster than Malia could read.

"Be careful," Chabela warned. "That machine tore a hole into the Underworld."

As if on cue, crazy whirring and sputtering noises rang out all around them!

WHIRRR! WHIZZZ! CHEEKA-POOKA-KREEK!

The room began to shake!

CHAPTER

MAPS AT LAST!

"Do something, geek squad!" Malia shouted.

Ivan put his hand on Dante's shoulder. "Exit BIOS, dude!"

Malia had no idea what he meant. But Dante's fingers danced across the keyboard. The screens went black. Then icons started popping up.

The room stopped shuddering. The noises faded.

Chabela clutched her chest, wheezing. "Don't give me a heart attack, *niños*."

"Sorry!" Dante said. "But look! There's an icon labeled portal grid."

"Open it, Dante!" Ivan shouted.

Dante clicked on it.

WHOOSH!

A map of the state filled the screens. There were dozens of glowing dots on it.

"Whoa," Ivan said, amazed.

"Can you zoom in on Gulf City?" Malia asked.

Ivan tapped the screen. Dante nodded. Thinking about their shared, secret language, Malia felt a sudden pang of guilt. She and Susana understood each other like that. Had Malia betrayed their friendship by lying to her?

"Okay, this should . . . ," Dante began.

WHIIIP!

The map now showed the streets of Gulf City.

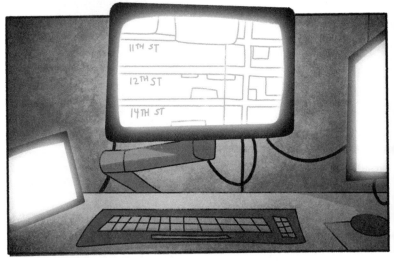

"Now," Dante said, "we're on 11th Street, so . . . ah, man!"

"What?" Malia asked.

"The alley portal is gone," Ivan explained, pointing at the screen. "They must disappear once we cross back to our world."

Malia squinted. "Scroll up, Dante. There! Where's that one?"

"That's the old canal," Chabela answered.

Malia pulled her tablet from her backpack. "Dante, can you send me the maps of the city and state?"

In a few moments, her tablet dinged.

"Now we control when and how we get to 13th Street," Ivan muttered. "Awesome."

"Okay, we have to hurry," Malia told Chabela. "Mickey has to find Bruno, then his return portal will open. He needs our help."

Chabela clasped her hands together. "I'll never be able to thank you enough, *niños.* Someday I will repay you."

"Well, it's almost Christmas," Dante pointed out. "I could send you a list of video games I've been . . ."

Malia gave him a little shove. "Come on, Pretty Boy. Let's rescue Mickey first."

Three chapters down! Are you ready to go back to 13th Street?

CHAPTER

SHARKS IN THE SEWER?

The cousins caught the next bus and got out near the canal.

Dante pinched his nose. "**PEW!** This stinks worse than the Snatch Bats' breath."

When they reached the edge of the canal, Malia checked the map. "This is it. Good thing our backpacks are waterproof."

Ivan made a sound like he might throw up. "Ladies first."

Malia shook her head. "Chickens. Follow my lead, as always."

She jumped into the slimy green water. As she sank, the warm canal water got colder.

Her feet touched something hard. As she tried to stand, her head burst from the water. Sopping spirals of hair hung all around her face.

Ivan and Dante popped up beside her.

"Wait, what?" Dante sputtered.

They weren't on 13th Street. They were **UNDER IT**.

"We're in a sewer,"

Ivan said. "A very big sewer."

"Or," said Dante, "the Underworld of the Underworld."

Ivan chuckled and Malia rolled her eyes.

In fact, the cousins were up to their stomachs in water inside a huge concrete tunnel. There were narrow walkways along each side. In the distance, metal ladders led to a catwalk or bridge.

Ivan pointed at one. "We should probably climb up there, then go through the manhole."

"Hmm," Malia mused. "Seems safer down here, though. Maybe we could—"

"Uh, boss?" Dante whispered. He sounded scared.

"What is it, Dante?" she asked.

"Sharks!" he cried.

Malia looked down at the water and saw six triangular fins heading right toward them!

"Run!" she screamed, splashing toward the

 28

nearest concrete ledge.

Ivan's longer legs helped him pull out in front. Dante was shrieking behind Malia, but she didn't dare look back.

Almost there! Almost there!

At last! She reached the narrow walkway. Ivan was clambering up. He helped her, too. They turned carefully and saw Dante swimming. The sharks were on his tail!

"Hurry!" Ivan shouted.

Dante moved his arms and legs in a wild flurry, but he was too slow!

The sharks lifted their heads from the water, jaws wide!

CHAPTER

BRUNO BITES!

Malia got ready to launch herself into the water and save her cousin. Then she noticed the sharks' eyes were glowing!

"That's . . . electricity," Ivan gasped.

Suddenly, a snarl echoed all around. Malia glanced up. A huge creature looked down at them.

Shaggy gray fur. Four legs. Big black eyes.

"Bruno!" Malia shouted.

The Irish wolfhound dove from the walkway! He hit the water between Dante and the sharks.

"Hold my hand, Ivan!" Malia shouted. "Anchor me!"

He did, and Malia leaned out over the water, reaching for Dante. When Dante grabbed her arm, she and Ivan pulled him up onto the narrow ledge.

The water churned and foamed. Bruno kept snapping at the sharks, which tried to zap him with electricity. But he was a ghost dog. Their shocks had no effect!

Soon their eyes went black, and the sharks swam away. Bruno dog-paddled over to the cousins, panting happily.

Dante slipped back into the water and gave the dog a big hug.

Bruno licked the boy's face, putting his big paws on Dante's shoulders.

"You're bigger than Dante, boy!" Ivan said, also returning to scratch Bruno behind the ears.

"How long have you been here?" asked Malia. "Mickey's looking for you, Bruno. You remember Mickey, right?"

Bruno barked, his tongue lolling between his teeth.

"Well, where is he, boy?" Dante asked. "Let's go find him!"

The Irish wolfhound gave Dante's face another lick before turning away and swimming off quickly.

Ivan looked at Malia with a question on his face.

"Don't ask me," Malia told him. "Follow that dog!"

CHAPTER

MEET THE PIKOS!

The cousins clung to Bruno's fur, letting him pull them along. After five minutes, loud splashing began to echo up ahead.

Bruno began to whine, as if someone he cared about was soon to arrive. The cousins held their breath.

The water started bubbling! Hands burst from the surface and . . .

. . . slapped spray into their faces!

A bunch of raccoon-like creatures began climbing out of the water, one atop the other. They made a weird, teetering tower of slick fur and lots of webbed hands.

They even had a webbed hand on their tails!

"HELLO, GUARDIAN!" shouted the creature at the very top. It was small, the size of Malia's cat. It had stripes and a white belly. "Ready for more partying?"

Bruno barked.

"Visitors?" cried the creature. "Yay! Pikos, you see. Who are you three?"

"Um, I'm Malia. This is Ivan and Dante. We're cousins."

The piko jumped into the air, spinning in a flip and straightening into a dive just before it hit the water.

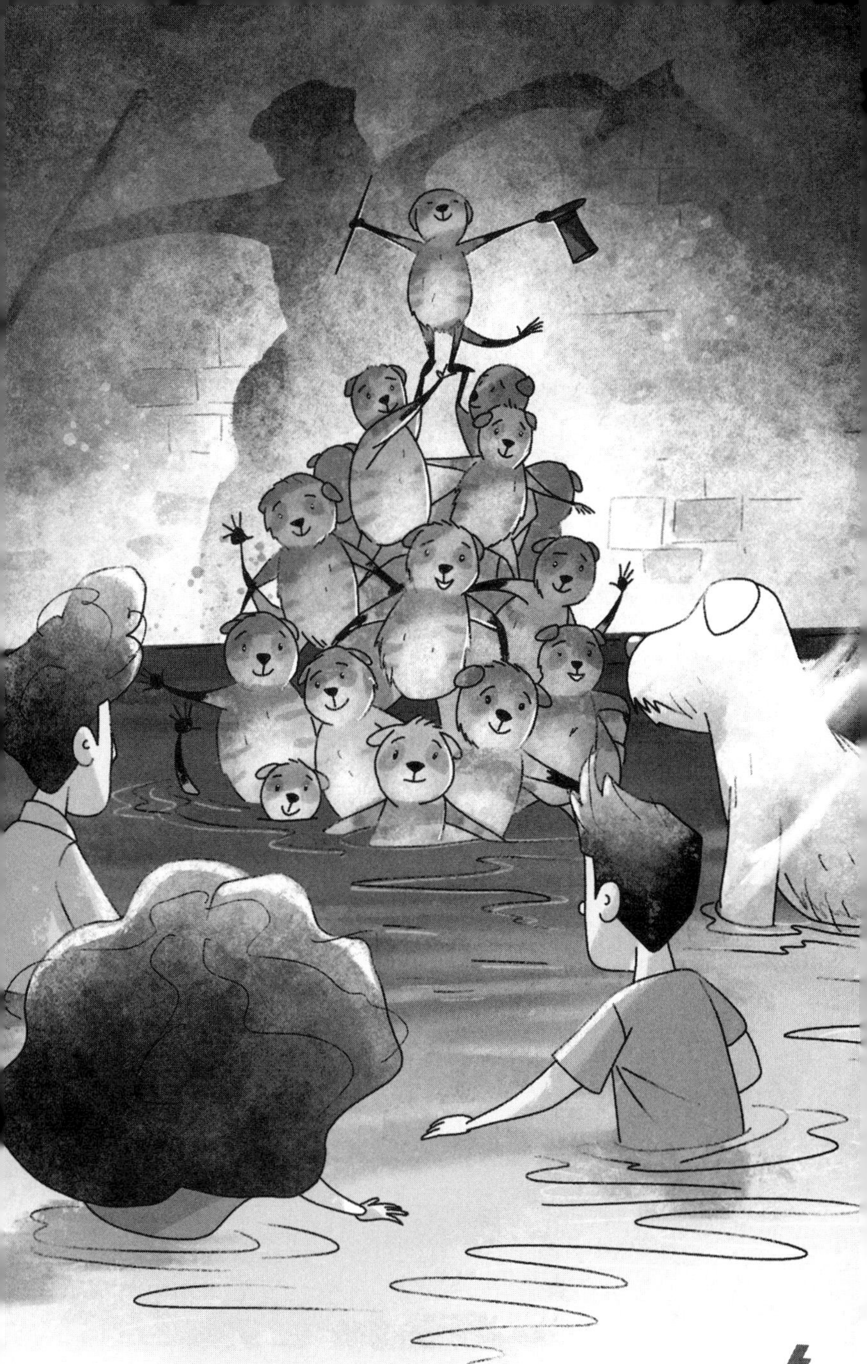

It popped up in front of Malia. "Hello, Cousins! Peki's my name! Want to play a tumbling game?"

"Actually, we just escaped some sharks, so . . . ," Malia began. But she couldn't finish, because all the pikos started snarling and moaning.

"Ew," said Peki. "Sharks hate pikos. Pikos hate sharks. Long story. Don't know where to start."

"Okay to play?" shouted all the pikos.

"Yes, yes. Go make a mess!" Peki said.

The tower tumbled apart. Dante laughed as the pikos began to wrestle in the water, leaping on top of each other. Some climbed onto Bruno's back and started dancing.

Peki jumped onto Malia's head.

"Better view," Peki said, laughing, "on top of you!"

Ivan pointed at the dog. "You called him Guardian."

"I did, indeed!" Peki said. "Since spirit dog has been around, shark attacks have gone way down."

"Well, your Guardian is named Bruno," Malia said. "He belongs to Mickey, the Quiet Prince."

Peki shuddered.

"This is bad," it said. "He'll be mad!"

¡Excelente! We found Bruno—and you read three more chapters.

CHAPTER

GROWLING GUARDIAN

"You mean you didn't realize you had the Quiet Prince's dog down here the entire time?" Ivan asked.

"No," Peki said. "I know you think we lied, but look—the pikos' brains are fried! We younger pups can speak, all right, but older ones just play and fight. It's the fault of the Shiver, who rule near the River."

"Who?" Malia asked.

"Do my words sound like barks?" Peki asked. "The Shiver's the sharks!"

"So every time you face the sharks," Ivan said, "the electricity makes the pikos less smart?"

"That's the truth," Peki said. "So we steal every tooth."

"Steal every tooth," muttered the other pikos.

Ivan wiped a tear from his cheek. "That's horrible. No wonder you need Bruno. If we can get the Quiet Prince here, though, Bruno will send him home and then stick around to keep you safe."

Peki smiled. "Well, that's okay! You saved the day!"

Malia looked down at the little creature.

"Can you find out where he is?"

"The flying frogs know all the gossip! I'll send a team to ask them what's up," Peki said. Then Peki gathered all the young pikos and gave them orders. Soon the group went swimming off.

Malia felt the tension leave her muscles. It would all be over soon. Mickey back home with Chabela. No more 13th Street. Maybe she could make things up to Susana and somehow find a way to tell her the truth.

Then something changed. The pikos started growling. Their slick fur stood up along their knobby backs.

Bruno snarled and barked.

"The Shiver, I fear," Peki whispered. "A bunch of them are here."

CHAPTER

8

SHOCKING SURPRISE!

Immediately, the pikos climbed onto Bruno's back, making a pyramid, like cheerleaders at a football game.

"Cousins!" shouted Peki. "Up you climb or you will die. The Shiver has at last arrived!"

Down the tunnel ahead of them came dozens of triangular fins. The sharks lifted their heads from the water.

Their eyes were glowing!

"Now!" Peki cried.

Malia didn't waste another second. She scrambled up the tower of slick piko bodies, getting as high as she could. Dante and Ivan followed. Just as their feet left the water, the sharks attacked!

BZZZZZZT!

Electricity forked like lightning from their eyes. The sewer water lit up! Balls of energy rolled along the surface, slamming into Bruno. The spirit dog staggered as waves hit him.

Then one of the bigger pikos lost its balance! Its tail dipped into the water, and it began to howl. Another piko reached down to help but got shocked as well.

After twenty seconds, the eyes of the Shiver went black.

But that wasn't the end!

WHOOOSH! WHIIISH!

They came swimming fast!

Peki clapped his front hands. "Okay, charge all gone again. Fighters, stay and help the Guardian. Rest of you, bolt! See you back at the holt!"

The pyramid came tumbling down. A dozen of the medium-sized pikos swept Malia, Dante, and Ivan down the tunnel.

The bigger ones crashed like a wave of grappling hands on the Shiver, pulling the sharks underwater. Bruno helped, slamming his big paws into the enemy and biting at their fins.

The pikos rushed through the sewer until they came to a broader chamber. There were two big concrete platforms on either side, nice and dry.

"Ah, it's their holt," Ivan muttered. "That's, like, their den."

"Den?" Dante said as he wrung water from  his shirt. "Where's the flat-screen and video game console, huh? Pikos, I swear. Worst hosts in the sewer."

CHAPTER 9

FLYING FROGS

The cousins were almost dry when the younger pikos returned. Gliding over their heads came four large bullfrogs. Malia blinked. A sort of parachute of thin skin stretched between the amphibians' legs.

"Like flying squirrels!" Ivan exclaimed.

Peki greeted his team. "Hey there, dudes! What's the news?"

Another little piko pointed at the frogs.

"These four frogs have confirmed that the Prince is down here."

"In the sewers?" Malia asked. "Where's he going?"

The frogs landed. The biggest one opened its mouth.

RIIIBIT!
CROOOOAAAAK!

"To the Lake at the End of the Street," the little piko translated.

"We've got to catch up with him," Malia said.

"Totally, boss," Dante said.

"By the time we arrive, it might be too late," Peki told the frogs. "Can you fly ahead and ask him to wait?"

GUH-ROOO!

Peki made thumbs-up signs with his front paws and tail. "That sound means yes, if you hadn't guessed."

"Thanks!" Malia told the frogs. They puffed up their necks and then hopped into the air, spreading their legs to catch a draft.

"This place gets weirder every time," Dante muttered.

You're more than halfway through the book! ¡Felicidades! (That means congratulations!)

CHAPTER

A SALTY SCHEME

"One catch I see," Peki said as the frogs glided away. "It's Shiver territory. Water's deep and dark. Lots of glowing sharks."

"Electricity is a problem," Ivan agreed. "If it jumps into us, we're toast."

Malia swallowed hard. "And no more pikos should suffer. It's not fair."

"Electricity," Dante said, trying to remember.

"Ms. Garay was just talking about it at the aquarium. What conducts a charge in the water is . . . uh . . ."

"Ions!" said Ivan. "From salts! Dante, you're a genius."

"Slow down," Malia said. "Explain."

Dante said, "Look, if there's just a little bit of salt in the water, electricity will jump into bodies. But if there's **A LOT OF SALT**—"

"The ions follow that easier path," Ivan finished.

Malia nodded. "So . . . if we made the water **REALLY SALTY**, the Shiver couldn't hurt us."

Peki clapped its hands excitedly. "And all pikos could stay and fight. Let the Shiver feel our might!"

Ivan petted Bruno for a moment, thinking. "This could work. But where could we get salt?"

"Listen to this," Peki said. "A plan with some risk."

"Risky is my middle name," said Dante, trying to sound brave.

Ivan winked at Malia before shouting, "¡*Uy*, *cucuy!*"

Dante jumped a foot into the air, shrieking in fear. When he noticed his cousins laughing, he shook his head and smiled.

CHAPTER

GLITCHY GETAWAY!

Peki led the cousins back to the metal ladders and the manhole.

"There's a store full of supplies," it said, "but also beady eyes."

Malia groaned. "Monsters."

"Nothing like that," Peki explained. "A bunch of rats."

Ivan cleared his throat. "Razor-clawed rats?"

"Radioactive rats?" Dante guessed.

Peki shook its head. "None of that weird stuff. Normal rats are bad enough."

The four of them climbed through the manhole. Peki pointed to a door with the two bars and three dots: number thirteen, a sign meaning people could enter.

Inside the store, cobwebby shelves were full of rusting cans. The cousins grabbed shopping bags and searched for the salt. When they found it, they filled their sacks.

BAM!
BAM!
BAM!

Malia jumped back as heavy forms dropped from the ceiling onto the shelves!

Rats! Dozens of them! Snarling and hissing!

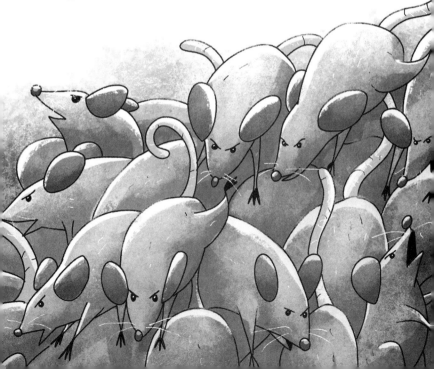

"Okay, that's disgusting," Dante said, backing away.

Malia felt her own stomach churning. "Yeah, let's get out of here."

The rats dropped to the floor, blocking the aisle.

"There's got to be another exit," Ivan said.

Peki scampered toward the wall. "Over here, if it please ya. There's a hole behind this freezer."

The cousins pushed the freezer aside and slipped through. They were not prepared for what was on the other side.

The room was

all dark gray, with lights flickering here and there before disappearing. A couch was stuck halfway in one wall. There was a sink in the ceiling. Ghostly forms kept stepping in and out of a doorway that looked like a baby had drawn it.

"An impossible room," Peki announced. "A shortcut soon."

"**THAT's** why only some doors are marked," Dante said. "It's like a video game. Places they don't expect you to go have incomplete code. They glitch."

Malia sighed. "Fascinating, nerd. Now how do we get out?"

Ivan scratched his head. "Maybe it'll glitch a door into existence?"

"That," said Malia, "is ridiculous."

"He's pretty close, despite your resistance," Peki said. "Except something will glitch *out* of existence."

Malia shook her head. She wondered how many other dangerous secrets 13th Street was keeping.

Then the floor disappeared, and Malia fell.

CHAPTER

12

THE SKULL SHIP

SPLASH!

Malia hit the water.

SPLISH!

SPLOSH!

SPLUSH!

Peki. Dante. Ivan.

Three of the older pikos were waiting nearby. They lifted the cousins out of the water and swam to the holt.

There Peki stood up on Malia's shoulder and addressed the pikos.

"Okay, friends; our journey begins! We head for the Lake despite the high stakes."

Dozens of pikos dove into the water and headed downstream. Bruno stayed out in front. Being a spirit dog, he would swim for a bit, then disappear, winking away. A few minutes later, they would find him dog-paddling happily many yards ahead.

He knew where they were going.
To his boy.

They searched for many hours with no luck. Suddenly Malia heard Bruno start whining excitedly.

"No way!" Dante exclaimed. "That is the coolest boat ever!"

Looking up, Malia saw what looked like the upside-down skull of a giant dragon. It was being crewed by chaneks! The little elves

were shooting vines at the walls of the sewer and pulling their bony boat through the water.

Standing at the front was Mickey Aguilar, his cape of black feathers flapping.

"Mickey!" Malia shouted, slipping off her piko's back and swimming closer. The Quiet Prince turned.

His eyes went wide when he saw the cousins.

"Stop the ship!" he called. "We have company."

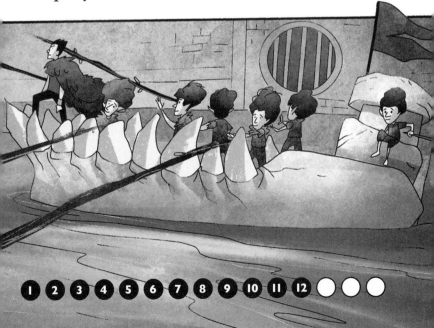

CHAPTER

13

BRUNO AND HIS BOY

"Why are y'all back?" Mickey asked. "Did my grandmother trick you again?"

Ivan shook his head. "No, she helped us. Dante pulled a map off your computer."

An excited bark made Mickey look straight down into the water.

Bruno winked away, reappearing on the boat right in front of the Quiet Prince. The

70

Irish wolfhound leapt onto Mickey, licking his face and whining.

Mickey was overwhelmed with happiness. He threw his arms around his dog's neck. "Bruno! Oh, my good boy! I've missed you so much!"

Bruno barked excitedly.

"Says sorry," one of the chaneks translated. Malia realized it was Shopal. "Was keeping pikos safe. Shiver's shocks make them forget much."

Mickey pressed his forehead against Bruno's snout. "Ah, you always were such a good boy. Don't worry. I'll use the Remember, **KAASK** spell on them. All their old memories will return."

Then it happened.

WHOOMP!

A portal opened right beside them.

"**NO!**" Mickey cried. "Not fair. I've been searching for almost five years!"

Dante pointed at the portal. "I know. But your parents are still looking for you. Your grandmother has gone *loca* trying to get you back."

"The whole point of this place," Mickey groaned, "was to spend more time with him!"

Malia sighed. "Then come back. You have the map. But right now? We risked everything to send you home. You'd better enter that portal, or I will get up there and kick you through."

Bruno nudged Mickey toward the portal with his snout.

Mickey gave his pet one more hug. "I won't be long, Bruno. Stay, boy."

He looked down at the cousins. "I'll never forget what you did for me, friends. Look for me on the other side. We have to stop her."

Malia narrowed her eyes. "Stop who?"

The portal hissed and started shrinking. Mickey gave his cape to his chanek allies. They bowed to him, and he bowed back.

"I'm called the Quiet Prince because this place has a noisy queen," Mickey said. "And she's stealing human children."

Without another word, Mickey stepped through the portal, back into the world he'd left behind.

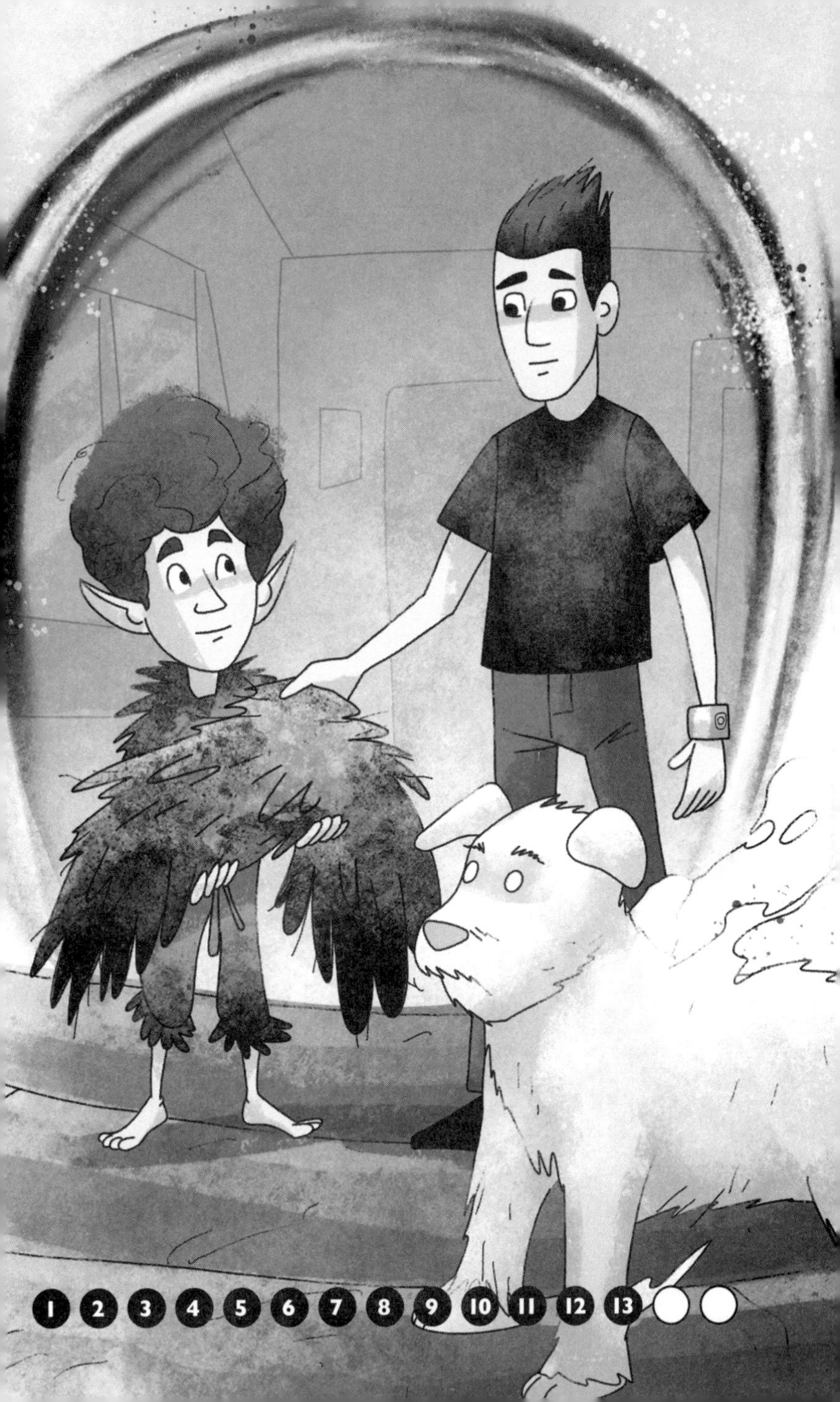
1 2 3 4 5 6 7 8 9 10 11 12 13

CHAPTER

14

MAGIC HANDS!

Malia couldn't believe what Mickey had said. Someone was stealing kids? Suddenly a horrifying hum filled the air, pulling Malia from her thoughts.

HMMRRRMM!

It was the Shiver! Their eyes were glowing as they attacked from all sides. A half dozen surrounded Malia!

She started
panicking. She
fumbled with
her bag, wanting
to dump salt
into the water

around her. It slipped from her fingers!

The pikos tried to reach her, but sharks kept knocking them away.

Then she heard Susana's voice. The girl was a morning person. Whenever they had sleepovers, Susana would wake Malia up with a sing-song voice.

Rise and shine, amiguita. *It's a brand-new day.*

Rise. Malia remembered. Mickey's spell.

As the sharks sent electricity sparking through the water, Malia laid her hands on the surface and shouted, **"RISE UP, SHE-WA!"**

The water around her burst upward! The sharks went flying away in every direction. Lightning bolts forked off into the air, fading fast.

As the water came crashing back in on Malia, the chaneks shot a vine out and pulled her onto the boat.

Frantic, Malia looked for her cousins. They were treading water, surrounded by pikos. Empty salt containers floated nearby.

The sharks attacked! They shot their electricity right at the boys and pikos—but it didn't touch them. The glow just flowed around them, drawn to the salt.

When the sharks' eyes went black again, pikos jumped on their backs. They slapped the hands of their tails against the noses of the Shiver. Hypnotized, the sharks opened their jaws wide and didn't move.

The chaneks pulled Ivan and Dante to safety aboard their boat. Then the pikos started snapping their magic fingers. With each snap, a tooth disappeared from their opponents' mouths.

"What in the world?" Ivan muttered.

"Pikos love teeth," Shopal said. "Like popcorn for them."

"Ugh," Malia groaned, disgusted.

"Dude," Dante said, "you're the one who dips her French fries in mayo, so don't judge."

The sharks had lost almost all their teeth.

WHOOMP!

Another portal opened up right above the water.

"Set your clocks to one thirteen," Malia told her cousins. "That's when we left our world. We will have been missing for an hour, if anyone checks."

"We still have to take the bus!" Ivan worried.

Shopal touched Malia's shoulder. "Child. Imagine destination. The portal will shift."

"Awesome!" Dante exclaimed. "The hallway, right outside our group's room in the aquarium?"

"Perfect!" Ivan agreed.

Malia tried to picture it. Then she grabbed her cousins by the hands, and the three of them jumped.

"Wait!" Dante shouted. "Shouldn't we change the time again?"

It was too late.

Don't stop now—you're almost at the end.

CHAPTER

CREEPY CLIFFHANGER

WHOOSH!

Malia opened her eyes. She was standing in the aquarium hallway and she was holding her cousins' hands.

With a shudder, she let go.

"We could've arrived right when we left!" Dante continued.

Ivan nodded. "He's got a point."

Malia groaned. "The portal was closing!"

"It's okay," Dante said. "The whole 'imagine destination' is a weird new twist. We'll get used to it."

"Ah, there you are!" cried Ms. Garay, coming around the corner. "The buses are waiting outside."

"S-sorry!" Ivan sputtered. "We had to use the restroom."

Ms. Garay put her hand on Malia's shoulder. "*M'ija*, why are your clothes damp?"

"Um, there was an . . . accident with the faucet," she lied.

Outside, Susana was waiting, her hands on her hips. "You owe me, Mal. I almost got in a bunch of trouble."

Ms. Garay was counting students. She

suddenly started rubbing her temples. "Oh dear. Now we're missing another two. Has anyone seen Santiago or Rafaela? Anyone?"

"Oh no." Ivan unzipped Malia's backpack and pulled out her tablet.

"Those better be the kitten photos," Susana muttered.

"Look!" he said. He had zoomed in on the aquarium. The others leaned in.

The map showed a new portal, fading away. "Mickey was right. It's happening to other kids now!"

Susana snatched the tablet from Ivan's hands and said, "Okay, enough is enough! No more secrets!"

Malia nodded. "You're right."

She reached up and put her hands on either side of her best friend's head.

"Remember, **KAASK**!"

Susana's eyes went wide. For a moment, Malia thought her friend might faint.

Finally, Susana spoke.

"Thirteenth Street. I remember!"

You survived the sharks! Good for you!

CONGRATULATIONS!

You've read **15** chapters,

87 pages,

and **5,134** words!

That's **SHOCKINGLY** awesome!

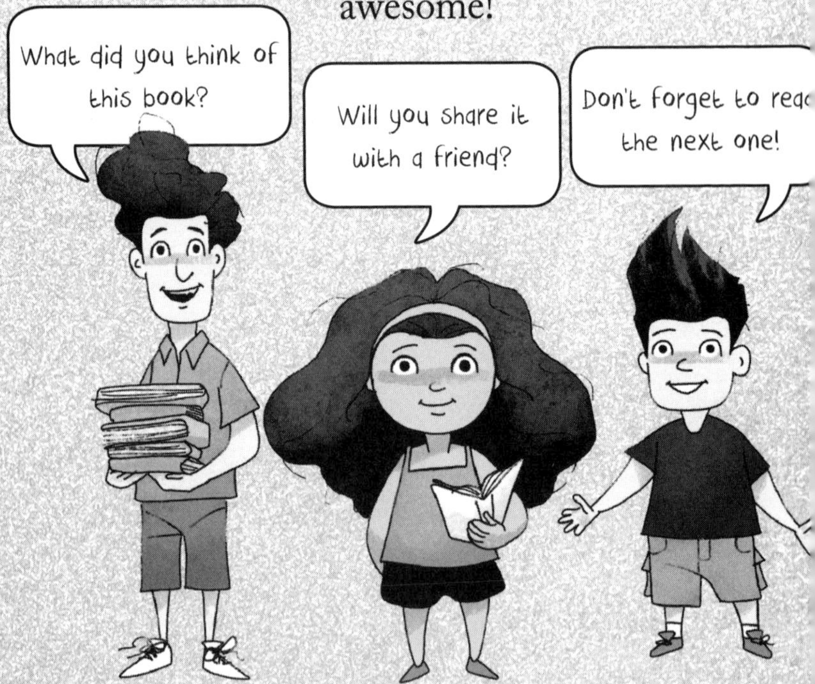
What did you think of this book?
Will you share it with a friend?
Don't forget to read the next one!

ACTIVITIES

THINK!

The cousins join forces with the pikos to bring Bruno to Mickey. Think of a time when you started on a new team and write about it.

FEEL!

Malia can't tell her best friend, Susana, the truth about 13th Street. How do you feel when you have a secret?

ACT!

Mickey finally goes home! Welcome back a friend or family member from a trip with a surprise card or video.

DAVID BOWLES is the award-winning Mexican American author of many books for young readers. He's traveled all over Mexico studying creepy legends, exploring ancient ruins, and avoiding monsters (so far). He lives in Donna, Texas.

SHANE CLESTER has been a professional illustrator since 2005, working on comics, storyboards, and children's books. Shane lives in Florida with his wonderful wife and their two tots. When not illustrating, he can usually be found by the pool.